# DON'T FEED THE GECKOS!

•• THE CARVER CHRONICLES ••

BOOK THREE

# DON'T FEED THE GECKOS!

BY Karen English

ILLUSTRATED BY
Laura Freeman

Houghton Mifflin Harcourt

Boston · New York

*For Gavin and Jacob and all their friends.*

*— K.E.*

*For my mom, who was stronger and braver*

*than she believed she was.*

*— L.F.*

Text copyright © 2015 by Karen English
Illustrations copyright © 2015 by Laura Freeman

www.hmhco.com

The illustrations were executed digitally.
The text was set in Napoleone Slab.

The Library of Congress has cataloged the hardcover edition as follows:

English, Karen.
Don't feed the geckos! / by Karen English ; illustrated by Laura Freeman.
pages cm. — (The Carver chronicles ; book three)
Summary: When Bernardo comes to live with Carlos temporarily, taking over his top bunk, his spot on the school soccer team, and even his Papi's attention, Carlos knows he is not happy, but worse, Bernardo starts messing with Carlos's pet geckos, so Carlos tries to see past his cousin's annoying ways and keep the peace for his family's sake.

[1. Cousins—Fiction. 2. Geckos—Fiction. 3. Schools—Fiction. 4. Hispanic Americans—Fiction.]   I. Freeman-Hines, Laura, illustrator. II. Title. III. Title: Do not feed the geckos!
PZ7.E7232Don 2015
[Fic]—dc23
2015013602

ISBN: 978-0-544-57529-5 hardcover
ISBN: 978-0-544-81083-9 paperback

Printed in the United States of America
DOC 10 9 8 7 6
4500710099

# • Contents •

# One
## Company Coming

Carlos's cousin, Bernardo, is coming. It's after school and Carlos sits down at the kitchen table to eat his Toaster Tart and eavesdrop on his mother and Tía Lupe's telephone conversation. His mother and Tía Lupe are always on the phone, checking with each other about everything. At least once or twice a day. His father doesn't even answer the phone anymore because he knows it's probably Tía Lupe.

Carlos overhears that his cousin Bernardo is coming to stay with them all the way from Texas because Bernardo's mom — Tía Emilia — is having a rough time and needs to get a fresh start somewhere else. She's moving to their town and sending Bernardo ahead.

Carlos stops chewing to listen better. Now it sounds

as if his mother and Tía Lupe are gossiping about Tía Emilia. She's always having problems; she doesn't make the right choices; she needs to manage her life better; and blah blah blah. Boring grown-up stuff. But it does make him think about his cousin and the fact that he's coming tomorrow.

His mother finally gets off the phone and comes to sit across from him. She puts on her serious face.

"Now, listen here, Carlos. Do you remember your cousin Bernardo?"

"A little bit." Bernardo was kind of chubby and had a mop of dark curly hair. Carlos went with Mami and Papi to Texas — San Antonio — when he was almost six and his sister, Issy (short for Isabella), had just turned three. It was Bernardo's birthday; Carlos turned six a few months after him. Carlos remembers sitting on a porch, eating a Creamsicle with Bernardo before his birthday

party. Oh, and running through the sprinklers. He remembers Bernardo cried because he wanted two pieces of birthday cake on his plate at once. He didn't want to wait until he finished what he had first. He just sat there crying and looking stupid with a mouth full of chewed-up cake.

And Carlos remembers seeing a photograph of Bernardo's dad in some kind of uniform — like an army uniform.

"Bernardo and Tía Emilia are moving here. Your *tía* wants him making the change in schools and settled as soon as possible. I'm picking him up tomorrow, so I just want to give you a heads-up."

*Maybe this will be a good thing. Maybe Bernardo will be cool and it'll be awesome to have another guy in the house — kind of like a brother.* They'll be able to do things together. Mami doesn't let Carlos go to the park by himself, or the store, or anywhere, actually. But with his cousin Bernardo here, he'll have an automatic buddy to go places with. *Yeah,* Carlos says to himself. *Bernardo.*

"What's he like?" Carlos asks.

"How am I supposed to know?" Mami says, sounding a little irritated. "All I know is that you better make your cousin feel at home. Make him feel welcome."

That's important to Mami, Carlos knows. Family. And sticking together and helping each other out.

Now Mami is giving him a list that she's counting out on her fingers — which shows she means business. She still has the serious face where she stares at Carlos, looking at him closely. His little sister comes into the room and stands next to Mami. She's wearing her tiara because she wants to be a queen when she grows up. It's annoying. Ever since Mami told her she was named after Queen Isabella of Spain, she's been wearing that tiara as much as possible. Mami did a report on Queen Isabella in high school, apparently.

"Can I have a Toaster Tart?" Issy asks in a whiny voice.

"Not now, Princess."

"Queen," Issy says. She adjusts her crown. Carlos rolls his eyes.

"Oh, right. *Queen* Isabella. Not now."

Issy must sense that there's something going on

that she wants to be a part of. She climbs onto Mami's lap, and then there are the two of them, looking at Carlos like they expect something special from him.

Bernardo has had a hard year, Mami tells him. She doesn't tell him what that means exactly, but because he has had this hard year, Carlos is to make Bernardo feel extra "at home." Like letting him feed Carlos's geckos. Stuff like that. "And introduce him to your friends, help him in school, share stuff with him."

That sounds super, but Carlos is stuck on letting Bernardo near his geckos. *Uh-uh...Ain't gonna happen.* At least not without supervision.

In the last few months, Carlos has discovered a love for animals — and insects. Different kinds of animals, like geckos and horned toads and albino snakes. He also realized he loves insects and their weird behaviors. Because of this, Carlos is no longer a member of the Knucklehead Club. He used to always miss turning in his homework, he did a sloppy job on his projects, he didn't always study for spelling tests, he brought toys to school to play with in his desk, and he didn't do his classwork in a timely fashion. Just a general knucklehead.

Those were the words of his teacher, Ms. Shelby-Ortiz, actually. He'd overheard her talking to Mr. Beaumont, the other third grade teacher, in the front office. She'd said, "I've got a few knuckleheads in my class this year. I'm hoping they'll decide to straighten up." She didn't know Carlos was listening.

He had come into the office to see if he could call his mother and tell her to bring the lunch he'd forgotten (typical knucklehead behavior), and he was standing right behind the two teachers as he waited his turn to speak to Mrs. Marker, the office lady.

He'd left after that. He didn't want Ms. Shelby-Ortiz to know he'd heard. He went back out to the yard and sat down on the nearest bench, thinking he'd just ask a couple of kids for whatever they could spare out of their own lunches.

It wasn't time to line up yet, so he'd had time to think — about being a *knucklehead*. He didn't want to be thought of like that. It made him feel funny. What if he went through his whole life being known as a knucklehead?

Besides, when he'd helped Papi fix the back door screen that Saturday, Papi had told him that if he wanted to be one of those new things he was talking about all the time — an entomologist or a zoologist — he'd have to go to college.

Could he get into college? Could he be an entomologist (a person who studies insects) or a zoologist (one who studies animals) while being a knucklehead? He didn't think so. That really bothered him.

# TWO
## Mami Still Talking

Mami is still talking — but once Carlos stops thinking about the knucklehead life, his thoughts return to Bernardo. Bernardo messing with his geckos: Darla, Peaches, and Gizmo . . . He doesn't think so. *Uh-uh.*

Carlos frowns. Just a little, so his mother doesn't really notice. Those geckos are fragile. They have to be taken care of just so. He barely lets Issy look at them. When Richard and Gavin come over and want to take one out of the terrarium and hold it, Carlos stands over them, watching closely so they don't scare the gecko or handle it the wrong way. Sometimes he'll only let them look at his geckos.

And then there's his ant farm. He's had that ant farm for three months. A person has to be especially gentle around an ant farm. No jiggling. Even a little jiggling can collapse a tunnel. Everything is especially sensitive in an ant farm.

You have to send for the ants after you get the farm. Which he did, though some were already dead on arrival. The information that came with the farm warned against just getting ants from any ol' place. If you weren't careful, you could get ants from two different colonies. Then they would fight each other. They wouldn't be cooperative and do the teamwork thing that ants do.

He'd carefully placed the farm on a little table in the corner of his room by itself. Just to ensure it wouldn't be exposed to any kind of jostling. Now, with Bernardo coming, he'll have to sit him down and explain all of this. He thinks about that. Didn't Bernardo breathe through his mouth and walk around with a kind of blank look on his face when he saw him last? Would he be able to grasp the words of warning?

The only way he allows Issy to look at the ants is if she sits in the little chair at the table where the ant farm is and keeps her hands folded. No touching, no pointing, no even breathing too hard on it. Just *looking*.

Soon he'll have his butterfly habitat, too. Papi said he could get one if he scored a hundred percent on the next five spelling tests. He has only two more to go. Then he'll be able to see the butterflies go from a larva (or caterpillar) to a chrysalis to a butterfly.

"What do you feed those things?" Richard asked one time when he and Gavin were over to practice soccer dribbles and they were looking at the geckos.

"Crickets."

"Yuck," Richard said. "Where do you get those?"

"At the pet store."

"Do you feed them with your hand, or do you just dump the crickets in?"

"Either way, but you have to be careful," Carlos had said.

"And the crickets are alive?" Gavin asked.

"Well, yeah."

There are so many things people just don't know about geckos.

● ● ●

Now, even though his mother is searching his face to see if her words are sinking in, Carlos is thinking, *No way. No way am I going to let that guy touch my geckos. Or my ant farm.*

Soon Mami's back to counting on her fingers: "I want you to put fresh linens on the top bunk."

"But that's *my* bunk, Mami."

Issy is smiling at him as if she's enjoying herself. Sometimes she likes to see Carlos flustered.

"I'm thinking Bernardo will probably prefer the top bunk — so let him have it." Mami pauses. "Clear out a dresser drawer so he'll have a place to put his socks and pajamas and stuff."

*Underwear,* Carlos thinks. He knows his mom means underwear too but just doesn't want to freak him out.

"Let me see. What am I missing?" Mami looks up toward the ceiling.

*That's enough,* Carlos wants to say.

"Oh, yeah. I want you to go up and give your bath-room a good scrubbing."

*Oooh. This is bad.* What his mother means by a good scrubbing, no kid should ever have to do. It means scouring the sink and tub, mopping the floor, and cleaning the *toilet.* Yuck! Who does he know who has to give a bathroom a good scrubbing? No one. That's what mothers are for. Not little kids. But his mother always says, "You mess up . . . you clean up." And she always has Papi onboard. He never disagrees with her. It's like he's obeying Mami as well. Then she usually tells Carlos all the chores she had to do as a kid — and Carlos thinks, *Oh, gosh, here it comes.*

"You think we had a dishwasher? What a joke. And a clothes dryer? I had to hang the clothes on a line with clothespins. You don't even know what a clothespin is, Buddy Boy."

Mami always calls him Buddy Boy when she's making a point about her childhood. She calls him Buddy Boy and his sister Miss Priss. Anyway, he does know what a clothespin is, because sometimes Ms.

Shelby-Ortiz uses clothespins to attach their artwork to an overhead string going from one end of the classroom to the other.

"And take him out in the backyard and let him kick around your soccer ball. Show him some moves. Make him feel like he's good at something. Your *tía* Lupe says some kids at his old school weren't very nice to him."

That gets Carlos's attention. Why were some kids not nice to Bernardo? What's with him? He almost asks this, but something tells him that it would just start up a long lecture from Mami about bullying and standing up for the bullied person and being careful not to blame the victim. So he keeps that question to himself.

Mami goes on. "You make sure your friends are nice to Bernardo. And the other kids in your class, too."

Carlos bites his lip. How's he supposed to do that?

"He's coming by himself?"

"Not exactly. Your *tía* Lupe's neighbor is coming here to visit some family. So she's bringing Bernardo with her."

"How are they getting here?"

"On the bus."

"Why not on an airplane?"

"Because not everyone's rich, Doofus."

That's another word Mami uses for Carlos. She called him that a lot after the last parent-teacher conference, when his parents learned he'd been acting up a little: messing up on spelling tests, playing with toys in his desk, and talking without raising his hand and waiting to be recognized. All that seemed natural before he turned over his new leaf. In fact, he once marveled at how kids like Nikki, Gavin, and Erik Castillo managed to keep it all together. They were the three best students in Ms. Shelby-Ortiz's class. And it didn't even seem hard for them. Scoring hundreds on spelling tests and multiplication-facts quizzes was nothing to them. It was probably like breathing for those three.

But now that he was being good, or at least better — paying attention, studying for spelling tests, and no longer bringing little toys from home to play with at every sneaky opportunity — he actually felt okay about comparing himself to Nikki and Gavin and Erik. He kind of looked at people like Calvin Vickers and Ralph Buyer with pity.

"How long's he here for?"

"For a while," his mother says, and Carlos thinks, *Funny how grownups can answer a question without really answering it. Like, how long is "for a while"?* It could mean anything: a few months; a few years.

"And he's going to be in my class?"

"Right."

"How long's a while?"

"Don't you worry about that, *mi hijo*. You just worry about the things you need to worry about."

Carlos frowns. What is it he's supposed to worry about? He definitely worries about soccer — that he's not very good at it. He wants to please Papi, but he can't really say he *loves* soccer the way Papi does. Carlos likes animals and insects more. (Not more than his mother and father and Issy in her tiara, but a lot). Sometimes, Carlos worries that he will never be chosen to be office monitor. And now he's worried about the next spelling test.

# Three
## Bernardo

**M**y cousin's coming," Carlos says to Richard and Gavin the next day while they sit in the cafeteria.

Richard is blowing bubbles into his carton of milk. When he finishes with that, he gulps down some air and lets out a big burp. He grins and looks around as if he's proud of his achievement.

"When's he coming?" Gavin asks.

"Today. After school."

"He's going to live with you?" Gavin asks.

"For a while."

"How long is that?"

"I don't know."

"What's he like?" Richard asks.

"I haven't seen him since I was little. He was kind of big and . . ."

"And what?" Gavin asks.

"And . . ." Carlos says again — but he can't put it into words. "It's hard to explain."

○ ○ ○

The bus station is crowded with travelers. Mami checks a paper in her hand and then looks up at the numbers above the doors of the idling buses. "Thirty-two . . . There it is," she says. She leads the way to a nearby bus.

People skip or slouch down the steps of the bus and then go wait by the luggage hold with their eyes peeled for their bags. Carlos watches the passengers. No Bernardo. At least no one who looks like the Bernardo he remembers.

Mami glances up at the bus's number again. "Yes. This is it." She watches the passengers as they go by, too. She checks her watch. Carlos glances down the rows between the idling buses. Then he feels a hand on his shoulder. When he turns around, there's Bernardo. Same face, but on a much bigger body. Still plump and kind of a blockhead, but half a head taller than Carlos. He's grinning widely.

"Hey, Carlos," he says. He's got a small bag of popcorn in his hand that he shoves into his canvas carry-on. Carlos thinks that Bernardo probably doesn't want to share. That's okay. Carlos wasn't in the mood for popcorn anyway.

"Hey, Bernardo," he says. Walking toward them is a woman with wire-rimmed glasses and a purple scarf around her neck, and lots of bags hooked onto both arms.

"Mrs. Ruiz?" his mother says.

The plump woman hugs Carlos's mother lightly. "This must be Carlos," she says, grinning down at him. "Boy, Bernardo's sure been talking about you."

"Really?" Mami says.

Carlos is surprised. He has only met Bernardo once — when he was five. What could Bernardo have been saying about him? They reach the parking lot, and Mrs. Ruiz sees the daughter who has come to pick her up. Mrs. Ruiz waves, hands Bernardo his luggage, and hurries to a small car. At one point, she looks back and says brightly, "He's all yours."

*What's that supposed to mean?* Carlos wonders. He looks over at Bernardo. He has a smug look on his face as if he's amused by some private joke.

Mami reaches down and gives Bernardo a hug. "My, what a big boy you've gotten to be," Mami says. Then she frowns as if she hopes Bernardo isn't taking that the wrong way — that he knows she was referring to height, not width. She turns to where she thinks she parked her car and leads the way, pressing the clicker thing on the key to sound the beep that will tell her where it is. Mami is always forgetting where she's parked.

Bernardo keeps grinning at Carlos and, with no warning, punches him in the arm — hard. It hurts. Carlos frowns and looks to his mother, but she's already walking briskly toward their car in the middle of a far row. He rubs his sore arm. He looks to Mami again, but she's no help. Somehow, that seems to signal the way it's going to be.

● ● ●

"Now, this is where you're going to sleep, Bernardo," Mami says. They're standing in the middle of Carlos's room while Mami pulls out the empty dresser drawer and shows Bernardo where he can put his clothes. She opens the closet and shoves Carlos's clothes aside on the rod. "You can put your clothes that need to be hung up in this closet, and Carlos is giving you the top bunk."

Carlos looks up at his sanctuary. That's his one spot — in the whole house. That's where he gets to play Hay Day (a video game with farm animals) without being bothered by Issy or his mother noticing and telling him to put that thing down and get a book. His top bunk is where he searches for information about weird animals or weird insects on his tablet. That's where he gets to imagine becoming either a zoologist or an entomologist when he grows up. Maybe both. That's where he gets to look down on his world and dream.

The world of his room, with the ant farm and the gecko aquarium and soon a butterfly habitat, is a reflection of him. It has *Carlos* written all over it. It contains everything he needs to relax . . . and to learn stuff that he can explain to Issy.

"A butterfly pops out of the furry worm?" she'd asked, when he was trying to explain the stages of a butterfly.

"No, there's another stage called the chrysalis stage."

"What?"

"You'll see." He didn't know how to explain the chrysalis stage.

His thoughts turn back to his future career. Maybe he can even get a Mason Bee house to hang from the maple tree in the backyard. He'll have to convince Mami about that one. He'll have to wait for the right time.

Just before Mami goes back downstairs, she turns to Carlos and says, "Go get Bernardo a towel and washcloth."

Carlos looks at Bernardo, who's standing in the

middle of the room, looking around. He hurries to the linen closet, grabs a washcloth and a towel, and when he comes back, he sees Bernardo peering into the terrarium.

"What are those?" Bernardo asks.

"Those are my geckos," Carlos says, his heart beating in his ears.

"Are they real?"

"Of course they're real."

"How come they're not moving?"

"That's what they do. They kind of look like they're posing. It's a defensive thing." He moves between the terrarium and Bernardo.

"But what's there to defend themselves from? There's just the three of them."

"It's just part of their behavior. They're programmed that way."

"What do you mean 'programmed'?"

Carlos searches for the words. It's difficult to explain.

"So what are their names?" Bernardo presses on.

"Darla is the one on the rock, Peaches is behind the

rock, and Gizmo is prob-
ably in his little cave thing."

"What kind of names are those?"
Bernardo turns to Carlos.

"Well, two are females and one's
male. I just came up with those names."

Bernardo makes a grunting sound. "What do they
eat?"

"Crickets, mostly. We get them at the pet store."

"And that's it? Sounds kind of boring."

Bernardo starts to reach into the terrarium, but
Carlos stops him. "Just leave them alone for now. I'll
let you hold one later."

Bernardo looks at Carlos for a moment as if he's
deciding whether to do as Carlos says. He looks back at
the terrarium, and a tiny smile plays on his lips.

Then he moves to the bunk bed, climbs the ladder, and perches himself in the middle of Carlos's bed.
"Hey, I like it up here."

Carlos had hoped that since Bernardo was on the
big side, he wouldn't want to climb up and down the
ladder. No such luck. He notices Bernardo is still wearing his shoes.

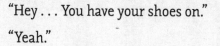

"Hey . . . You have your shoes on."

"Yeah."

"You can't sit on my bed with shoes on."

"How come?"

"Just take them off before you get on my bed."

"It's *my* bed now."

What can Carlos say to that? Thanks to Mami, it *is* his bed.

● ● ●

"So, Bernardo," Papi says at dinner, "you think you'll like it here?"

Bernardo takes a bite of his lime chicken. He chews and swallows. "My mom makes this with cilantro," he says to Mami. Then he turns to Papi. "It's okay. I guess I have to see. I'm going to miss my friends."

"Did you have a lot of friends in Texas?" Mami asks.

"Yeah. I had a lot of friends."

Carlos glances at Mami, to see if she believes him. But Mami's face doesn't show much.

"What else are you going to miss?"

"I'm going to miss my soccer team."

"Oh. Soccer," Mami says.

"Yeah, and they're going to miss me, too. 'Cause I score most of the goals."

"Wow," Mami says. "Now, that's interesting. We need a good soccer player for Carlos's team."

*What does Mami mean by that?* Carlos wonders. Just because he's had a few bad games, that doesn't mean she should count him out.

"Well . . . we're going to try real hard to make you feel at home. Right, Carlos?" Mami says, turning to him.

"Yeah," Carlos agrees.

Suddenly Bernardo is squirming in his seat. "I need to go to the bathroom," he says.

"Sure, go ahead," Mami says.

After Bernardo leaves the table, Mami turns to Carlos. "I'm going to talk to Coach Willis and see if Bernardo can be on the team. I think that will make him feel even more at home. Don't you think that's a good idea, Carlos?"

Carlos can't really think just then. He's busy listening to the sounds upstairs. Did Bernardo really need to go to the bathroom? Could he be in Carlos's room, messing with his geckos or his ant farm?

"Carlos?"

"Huh?"

"What do you think about Bernardo being on your soccer team?"

"Yeah, yeah — okay."

"What's that supposed to mean?"

Carlos is almost certain he hears steps above his head in his bedroom. "I mean, yeah, that's fine, Mami." He takes a sip of milk. "Can I go to the bathroom too?"

"Wait until Bernardo comes back."

"But I can use your bathroom."

Mami sighs. "Okay," she says. "Don't be up there all year."

# Four
## You Can't Feed a Gecko Popcorn!

**C**arlos takes the stairs two at a time. He nearly bumps into Bernardo just as he reaches the landing. Bernardo smiles and reaches back as if to give Carlos a punch. Then he drops his hand and laughs.

Carlos watches after him until he disappears down the stairs, and then ducks into his own room. He checks the ant farm. All the tunnels seem to be undisturbed. The ants are still busy doing ant things. Then he turns to the terrarium and spots several kernels of popcorn on its floor. A kernel has been placed on top of Gizmo's cave!

His breath quickens; his fists clench. He can't believe it. *Popcorn!* Luckily, the geckos have ignored the food. Probably because they can't chase it around the terrarium. Maybe they thought the popcorn was some kind of plant.

Whatever the case, Carlos storms down the stairs, marches into the dining room, and says to Bernardo, "You can't feed a gecko popcorn!" He feels his face grow warm. He knows he must be red from the neck up.

"What?" Bernardo turns to him, his eyes wide with innocence.

"Don't say you didn't put popcorn in the geckos' terrarium." Carlos waits. He can't believe Bernardo would try to lie.

Bernardo looks at Mami. Mami is looking back and forth between Carlos and Bernardo. He drops his head and raises his eyebrows forlornly. "I thought they'd like it."

"What?"

"Yeah, I was feeling kind of sorry for them, 'cause all they ever get is crickets. Crickets, crickets, crickets. I know I'd get tired if all I ever got was crickets."

"You're not a gecko! They're very special creatures. You can't just give them any ol' thing!"

Carlos looks to Mami with a helpless expression.

"Carlos, don't make such a big deal of it. No harm done," she says.

Carlos looks to his father. Papi shrugs. "They're still alive, right?"

Carlos takes a big, deep breath and lets it out slowly. He can't bring himself to speak. He hunches over his plate and resumes eating, but he's lost his appetite.

● ● ●

Later, while Mami does the dishes, Papi takes Bernardo out in the backyard so Bernardo can show him what he's got . . . soccerwise. Though Carlos is all the way up in his room studying his multiplication facts, he can hear Papi and Bernardo dribbling the soccer ball back and forth between them.

"In this dribble, remember to connect with the ball using the inside of your foot, and stay on your toes,"

Papi is saying to Bernardo. Then Carlos hears, "Good! You're a natural."

Carlos marches over to his open window and closes it. He doesn't want to hear anything positive about Bernardo just now.

Later, after homework and his shower, when Carlos goes downstairs to get ice cream and watch basketball with Papi, he hears Mami saying to Bernardo, "Yeah, the team is kind of struggling right now, and I have a feeling you'll be a great addition."

She and Papi and Bernardo are sitting in front of the basketball game, eating ice cream. Carlos doesn't get it. Is anyone going to notice that he's there? Even Issy, sitting cross-legged on the floor, doesn't look up from her coloring book. What's wrong with this family?

And what does Mami mean that the team's been struggling? He flops down into the easy chair facing the TV. He pokes out his lower lip a little bit — enough

to let everyone know that he's still annoyed about the popcorn. The problem is, no one seems to notice.

● ● ●

Bernardo just won't go to sleep. He hasn't bothered to take his shower yet or brush his teeth, and now he's up there on the top bunk, playing his loud video game, with his legs hanging down practically in Carlos's face. Carlos has to get to sleep. He's exhausted, and he doesn't want to be tired at school the next day.

"Are you going to take your shower and brush your teeth? I'm finished with the bathroom."

"Why should I do that?"

"You don't brush your teeth before you go to bed?"

"No. I brush 'em in the morning. If I have time."

"Oh," Carlos says. He waits a few minutes, then says, "How long you think you're going to play that video game?"

"Asphalt Eight? I don't know. I'm not sleepy, so . . ."

"But you're tired, right?"

"Not really."

Carlos closes his eyes and tries his best to go to sleep. Just when he thinks he can't stand the noise of the game any longer, Bernardo turns it off and falls back on the bed. It's quiet. Finally.

But before long, just as Carlos is drifting off, he hears snoring. Bernardo has fallen asleep, but he's snoring like a bear.

*Oh, no,* Carlos thinks. *This is torture.*

He has to admit that so far Bernardo is kind of a disappointment. And Carlos cannot forget that punch.

# Five
## First Day

As soon as they enter the schoolyard, Mami, Issy, and Bernardo go one way, to the office, and Carlos goes another, to his line. He feels relieved.

"That your cousin?" Gavin asks as Carlos slips into the line behind him. They have to wait for Ms. Shelby-Ortiz to pick them up from the yard. They're supposed to be standing like soldiers, hands to themselves, mouths zipped, facing straight ahead. Gavin, Richard, and Carlos watch Carlos's mom walk Bernardo into the school building.

"He's kinda . . . *big*," Gavin says.

"Yeah," Carlos agrees, rubbing his shoulder absently.

"What's he like?" Richard asks.

"Hard to say."

"He's going to be in *our* class?"

Carlos nods. "Uh-huh."

●  ●  ●

The first thing Carlos notices when he enters the classroom is that there's an open topic for morning journal. "Yes!" he says under his breath. He's got a lot to say. Stuff he wants to get out. He's probably the only one of the four students at Table Two who likes to write. In the past, writing was always a big groan. A struggle. But for some reason, it's getting easier and easier. He simply writes what he'd say if he was explaining out loud something that happened to him. He just has to remind himself to go over his work to see if it's okay. Ms. Shelby-Ortiz has told everyone that they should read their journal entries to themselves when they think they're finished. That's the way to catch the mistakes and to see if what they've written is clear. It will help them get rid of all those pesky run-on sentences and confusion.

Carlos takes out his pencil and begins:

My cousin Bernardo is here. At my house. He's going to stay with us a while until his mother gets here and picks him up. I don't think Bernardo has a father anymore. I want to ask him, but I think I'll wait. Mami will just tell me its not my bizness. Maybe he was in the army or something and didnt make it. Or something. I don't know if I like Bernardo. He has a funny personallity. I think hes kind of sneaky. And I don't like that he gave me a punch on the arm for nothing when I first met him. I didnt do nothing to him. Nothing. And he just punched me hard on the arm. My arm is still sore. I didn't tell because I didnt want him too get in trouble but he better not do that again just because hes bigger than me. I dont know how long he's going to be with us. Well, that all I got to say about Bernardo. Oh and hes bigger than I am and a little older than I am. Oh and he fed popcorn to my geckos. He could have made them choke. Now I'm kind of worried about my geckos. Because he's in my room and he has the top bunk. Thats not even fair.

Carlos reads over what he's written under his breath. It sounds good. He looks around. Almost everyone is still writing. He knows he should take out his Sustained Silent Reading book, but he chose the wrong one. It's really boring. He'd like to get another book, but Ms. Shelby-Ortiz says you need to give some of them a chance. Stick with them, because they can start out boring and then get good later.

Sometimes Mami will say, "Go in your room and read and don't come out for thirty minutes." Then she'll warn, "And if I catch you playing with a video game or looking up something about some animal, I'm going to have you sit at the kitchen table and read right in front of me. And I'm going to take that video game and you won't see it for a month."

Sometimes he wonders if mothers just think up stuff to make kids miserable. When she says this to him, he'll go into his room, feeling like he's being punished. He'll start reading, but before long his mind will be wandering all over the place. Just on its own. He'll think of soccer — the different ways to pass the ball—then he'll start looking at the video game on his dresser, wanting to play it so bad.

While he's reading, the video game will keep popping into his mind. Or he'll remember a pass he messed up during the last soccer game.

Mami will call out, "How you doing up there with *Sign of the Arrow?*"

And he will say, "Fine." But he won't be doing fine, because Mami got the book from the library and read

it herself, and there will be questions. Detailed questions.

She'd loved *The Sign of the Arrow* when she was little and told him, "You'll love it, too." And he'd believed her. "For one thing, it's a boy book, and it has a lot of adventure," she'd said. Yeah, he could tell by the picture on the cover of a boy hiking along some mountain trail that it was going to have adventure.

But the adventure has been slow to build up, and he keeps skipping pages, looking for the good part. He skips ahead for a few pages, goes back to where he left off, and tries to remember what happened.

Soon, he'll hear his mother call up to his room with, "Come here, Buddy Boy. I need you to summarize chapter three for me." He'll come down to the kitchen, taking his time, and sit across from her while she's got her nose in chapter three, waiting for him to summarize it. And there he'll be, trying hard to remember what happened in chapter three.

"That's what I thought," she'll eventually say. "Get back up there and read chapter three *again*," and he'll think, *Ughhh*. Why couldn't books be like video games? Fast moving. Exciting. He doesn't say that out loud, but that's what he says in his head.

● ● ●

"Who's that guy?" Carlos hears Rosario ask. She sits across from him at Table Two. He follows her gaze to see Bernardo, Ms. Shelby-Ortiz, and Mami standing together near the door. Mami has Issy by the hand. She's being extra good. Ms. Shelby-Ortiz and Mami are talking, and Bernardo looks like he's sizing up the classroom. He moves over to the jigsaw table and stares at the puzzle of extinct species, which is nearly finished.

Room Ten is proud of the one-thousand-piece jigsaw puzzle. It's the first time the class has worked on one with a thousand pieces. Ms. Shelby-Ortiz has promised that when it's all finished, she'll put that special jigsaw puzzle glue on it and then she'll hang it on the wall — by the door, so all the kids from the other classes can see it when they walk by.

"Class," Ms. Shelby-Ortiz says. She holds up one hand and puts her finger over her mouth with the other. Everyone else does the same to show that they are listening, including Carlos. Then they all put their hands down. Everyone is quiet — showing Ms. Shelby-Ortiz that they have their listening ears on.

"We have a new student." She beams to drum up enthusiasm. "We're all going to show Bernardo here what a great place Carver Elementary School is. Right?"

Some kids nod slowly. Some say, "Yes, Ms. Shelby-Ortiz." Some look at Bernardo skeptically. His T-shirt hangs out, and his hair looks a little messy. Carlos notices that, once again, he's breathing through his mouth — and when he remembers to close it, it's set in kind of a sneer. Carlos scoots down a little in his chair and looks out the window. But soon he hears his name.

"Carlos, I'm going to let you take Bernardo under your wing and show him the ropes: where the bathroom is, the cafeteria, et cetera, et cetera. He can have one of the empty cubbies for his lunch and book bag, and"—she claps her hands and looks around—"the pencil sharpener rules ... He'll need to know those and also the rest of the class rules. In fact, Richard, switch to the empty desk across from Antonia and let Bernardo have yours."

Bernardo stands there waiting. His eyes look a little distant, as if he's bored with all this introduction stuff.

"That's your cousin?" Carlos's tablemate, Ralph, whispers to him.

Carlos nods.

"Where'd he come from?"

"Texas."

"Where the cowboys live?"

"I guess," Carlos says, imagining cowboys and horses and lassos. He sees Mami and Issy leave.

"How long is he going to be here?"

Carlos had been putting rubber markings on the top of his desk with the edge of his pink eraser. Now he begins to clean them away. He looks up at Ralph. "For a while," he says.

Ms. Shelby-Ortiz begins pulling materials and

books that Bernardo will need from the shelf near her desk. She signals for Carlos to give her a hand. She piles books into his arms, and Bernardo's arms too. There are also workbooks and a cardboard pencil box and a morning journal and spiral notebooks. All of this is carried to Bernardo's new desk right next to Carlos's.

Ms. Shelby-Ortiz comes over with a brand-new name tag for Bernardo. She removes Richard's name tag and tapes Bernardo's to the upper right-hand corner of his desk. It's as if Bernardo has even moved into Carlos's space at school. It's like they're joined at the hip, the way some identical twins are born. Carlos just can't get away from him.

Ms. Shelby-Ortiz consults her plan book. "Okay . . . We still have time to finish up our morning journals before reading. Carlos, will you explain to Bernardo what we do with our morning journals?"

Carlos pulls the fresh new journal out from the pile of books — books Bernardo has made no effort to place inside his desk — and says, "This is your morning journal. Every day after we put all our stuff away, we check the board for the topic, and then we write on that topic." Carlos points to the board. Bernardo glances toward it. His face is blank. He looks as if he didn't get enough sleep the night before. Which is strange, because Carlos is the one who didn't get enough sleep. He had to listen to Bernardo snoring almost all night long.

"See, today is open topic. That means you can write about anything you want."

Bernardo suddenly perks up. "What did you write about so far?"

"Me?"

"Yeah."

Carlos doesn't really want to say. There's some stuff that Bernardo might not find too flattering. "Oh . . . I just wrote some stuff, you know. About the weekend."

"Can I see it?"

"Uh, we don't have that much time, and sometimes Ms. Shelby-Ortiz has us pass them in so she can check them over. Better get started."

Bernardo opens his brand-new morning journal. He looks over at Carlos's. Carlos has decorated his with bugs and animals. Bernardo sits there, staring.

Then he picks up his pencil and looks at the lead.

He tests its sharpness on his finger. He opens his journal to the first page.

"Put today's date in the upper right-hand corner. That's what Ms. Shelby-Ortiz tells us to do."

Bernardo looks up at the board to see the date, then proceeds to write it in the upper right-hand corner of the page. He has to look up several times to get the spelling right. Carlos can hear him breathing through his mouth. Carlos takes out his book that he's "reading for pleasure" and opens to where he left off.

A few minutes later, Ms. Shelby-Ortiz is saying, "Okay, class, pencils down. Rosario, collect the journals for me." Carlos looks over at Bernardo's open journal. There are only a few lines written in large, messy print. He's not surprised.

# Six
## All the Best Kickers

**R**ecess is better, because Room Ten has the kickball and jump rope areas, and Carlos doesn't have to watch over Bernardo. He only has to point out the boys' bathroom when Bernardo needs it and send him on his way.

Carlos wants to be on Ralph's team. If Ralph played soccer, he'd be one of the best kickers on the Miller's Park soccer team. Calvin Vickers is the other team captain, and somehow Carlos knows Calvin's going to pick him.

As Room Ten's players stand in a group, waiting for Calvin to pick his first teammate, Carlos mutters quietly, "Don't pick me . . . Don't pick me."

"Carlos," Calvin Vickers says.

Carlos sighs and goes to stand behind him.

Ralph calls out, "Emilio."

*Another good kicker,* Carlos thinks.

Calvin calls out, "Gavin."

"Shoot," Carlos says under his breath, and watches while Gavin makes his way over and gets behind him. Gavin may be good on his skateboard, but he's only so-so at kickball.

Richard gets on Ralph's team, and that gives Ralph's team the advantage with three good players. Calvin spies Bernardo walking across the yard, returning from the boys' bathroom.

"Okay, we'll get the new guy," he says.

Carlos looks to see Bernardo lumbering across the yard to the baseball diamond they use for kickball. *Oh, no,* he thinks. *This is not good.*

Bernardo trudges up to Carlos. "What are you guys doing?"

"Choosing up sides for kickball," Carlos says. "You're on my team."

"Cool," Bernardo says. He looks confident.

Ralph and Calvin keep choosing up sides until each team has six players.

"Play ball!" Bernardo yells, and everyone turns to stare at him.

"I just like saying that," he explains, and then looks down, grinning at the ground.

● ● ●

The teams flip a coin to see which will kick first. Ralph's team wins. *More bad luck,* Carlos thinks. Ralph chooses himself to be the first kicker. No surprise there. He wants to start off the game with his team on top.

"Hey, let me pitch!" Carlos yells to Calvin, who's looking over his team. "I always get it over the base." Calvin checks him for a second, then tosses the ball to Gerald. "You pitch, Gerald."

Carlos's shoulders slump. He knows Calvin is still mad because Carlos didn't let him cheat off his paper last week during the spelling test. Carlos shrugs and finds a place near first base. Bernardo saunters to third. The other team members spread out over the field.

Gerald pitches a slow, easy roll, and Ralph kicks a high ball straight between second and third. It lands right in Bernardo's outstretched arms. "Out!" he cries.

Ralph looks at Bernardo for a moment and then slinks over to the bench. He seems a little surprised.

Before Ralph sits down, he switches places with Emilio so that he can quickly have another shot at kicking. For some reason, Emilio doesn't seem to mind. The other players let this go as well. Too many squabbles can cut into play time. The next ball Gerald rolls is a bit wobbly and goes a foot to the left of home base. Carlos would have done better at pitching.

"Ball!" Ralph yells out, using a baseball term.

Gerald pitches again. The ball rolls wide of the mark once more, and Ralph doesn't even try to kick it.

"Ball two!" he yells out.

Carlos slaps his forehead. *What a team!* "Hey, Gerald! How about getting it over the base?"

Gerald whips around and bounces the ball once — hard. "You think you can do better?"

"Yeah!"

Gerald ignores him and pitches the ball fast and wild. It doesn't even go near home base.

Carlos takes in a deep breath. "Ball three!" Ralph cries. "One more and I walk!"

"Let me pitch, Calvin!"

Calvin looks Carlos up and down. "Okay." He turns toward Gerald. "You're on first!"

Gerald bounces the ball low and hard to Carlos and stomps to first base. Carlos grabs it like he doesn't even notice his fingertips are stinging, then takes his place at the pitcher's spot and rolls the ball fast — with no bounces — and catches Ralph by surprise. Ralph is all ready to call out "Ball four," but he doesn't have a chance. The ball is crossing the base, leaving him barely enough time to get into position.

His foot slips across the ball, and he nearly stumbles kicking it. It goes nowhere, but Ralph runs toward first base anyway. Erik Castillo, behind home plate, grabs the ball and throws it toward Bernardo, just as Ralph is rounding first and heading toward second base. Bernardo is right where he needs to be. He catches the ball, runs to second, and stomps on the base before Ralph can reach it.

"That's two outs!" Bernardo cries. He bounces the ball once — hard — to emphasize his point. Carlos is impressed, but not really surprised. Even though Bernardo's kind of big, that doesn't always mean a person won't be athletic. Bernardo's big — *and* a good kickball player.

That's what Carlos tells Papi in the car after school. Usually Mami picks him up, but she has a dentist appointment, and Papi has a day off from work for some reason.

Carlos goes on. "If it wasn't for Bernardo, we would have lost. Because not only was Bernardo good in the field, he was a good kicker."

"Really?" Papi says. He checks Bernardo in the rearview mirror. Bernardo's busy looking out the window, as if he has other things on his mind.

Carlos is a little disappointed. He thought pumping up Bernardo to Papi would make Bernardo act nicer later — at home. But Bernardo doesn't even seem to notice.

"Wow," Papi says, seemingly impressed.

"I'm good at all sports," Bernardo says out of the blue. Carlos feels a bit irritated.

"You can't be good at *all* sports," Papi says.

"Well, the important ones."

Carlos glances at the back of Papi's head, wondering what the expression on his face is right now. Carlos is sure that Papi will have a response to that.

"Every sport is important to the people who play them," Papi says.

"Well, I'm talking about the main sports, like baseball and football and basketball . . . and soccer. I'll probably play on Carlos's team. I think they're going to need me."

Carlos thinks maybe Bernardo's gotten his hopes up too quickly. "Mami hasn't spoken to Coach Willis yet," he says.

Bernardo just shrugs. "You'll see."

● ● ●

The snoring continues — right above Carlos's head. He sits up. He rubs his eyes. How's he going to live with that noise? Now it kind of sounds like an animal's low growl with something choppy at the end. There's a little bit of smacking, too. Carlos waits. He knows it's not

going to stop. How can Bernardo sleep through his own snoring?

After fifteen minutes of staring at the bottom of the upper bunk, fifteen minutes of waiting for it to stop, Carlos reaches under his bed for his hockey stick. He jams the underside of the bunk, hard.

It takes a couple of jabs before Bernardo sits up. "What, what? What's going on?"

"You're snoring!"

"What?"

"You're snoring and waking me up!"

Bernardo drops his head over the edge of the bunk. "No, I'm not. I don't snore."

"Yes, you do!"

"I don't see how that's keeping you awake."

"It's *loud!*"

"Then just close your ears."

Carlos jumps out of bed and stomps to the bathroom, not caring if he wakes up the rest of the family. He grabs some toilet paper, pulls it apart, then balls up each half and stuffs it into his ears. He climbs back in bed and lies there for a moment, listening. Quiet . . . it seems at first, but then the snoring gets through the tissue. It's muffled, but still there. He stares at the underside of the top bunk. Bernardo's back to sleep. How can that be? How long is Carlos going to have to put up with him?

# Seven
## The Care and Feeding of Geckos

The next thing Carlos knows, Bernardo is shaking him awake and saying, "Let me feed the geckos."

It's morning. Carlos covers his eyes. "Let me wake up." He yawns.

"Come on, come on!"

Carlos pulls himself up and climbs slowly out of bed. He moves to the terrarium and stands there a moment, still waking up. Bernardo bends down to look through the glass. "Let me hold one."

"I have to give you the rules first."

"Okay, give me the rules, then."

"First, I need to tell you about geckos."

Bernardo seems suddenly bored. He looks as if he just wants to get his hand into the terrarium.

"First of all," Carlos says, "you don't play with geckos more than thirty minutes a day, and that's mainly just holding them."

Bernardo says, "Yeah, yeah . . . okay."

Carlos studies him for a few seconds. "We'll take turns feeding them. I always feed them in the morning, so you can watch me."

"Just show me how it's done," Bernardo says.

"I'm going to tell you about the geckos and the ants. And you better listen." This is going to be hard — keeping Bernardo from traumatizing his geckos or causing tunnel collapse in his ant farm.

"I'm going to start with the ant farm because it's the most . . . Well, things can happen."

"Like what?" Bernardo asks.

"Well, see all those tunnels they've made?"

Bernardo practically drools as he peers through the glass.

"They go to a lot of trouble to make them. That's why even Issy is careful when she's near the ant farm table. If this table is jiggled, you can collapse their tunnels. And they'll get buried."

"How long do they live, anyway?"

"Why?"

"Just wondering how long an ant lives."

Carlos looks at Bernardo suspiciously. The question bothers him.

"Well, that's the thing. They don't live all that long." He points out a small section of the farm near the surface. "See this here?"

Bernardo lowers himself some more, but then wobbles a little on his feet. Carlos yanks him back by his shirt collar.

"Hey!"

"I said you have to be careful around the farm!"

"I'm being careful!" Bernardo straightens.

"I was going to say, that little section is like their graveyard. It's called a midden. They carry the dead ants to it."

"An ant graveyard?" Bernardo's eyes widen. He looks back at the geckos. "Do the geckos have a graveyard?"

"No. They live longer. Pay attention."

Bernardo stares into Carlos's eyes to show he's

paying attention, but an expression crosses over his face that makes Carlos feel a little uneasy.

Carlos explains how the ants in the farm are western harvester ants, and they eat just about anything, but a little bit of cracker crumbs and some drops of water dripped onto the sand will do. Also, whatever they don't eat has to be taken out of the farm because it will get all moldy. Bernardo is beginning to look bored. Carlos knows Bernardo's just waiting for him to finish.

"Can I feed 'em too?"

"We'll get to that. If I think you can be careful, I'll let you feed them in a minute. Now, here are the gecko rules, so listen carefully."

"Gecko rules."

"Here's what you need to know."

Bernardo waits.

All Carlos can think is, *Can I trust this guy?*

"What are the rules?"

"Okay, first, they're leopard geckos . . ."

"That's why they have the spots."

"Right. And two are female," he reminds Bernardo.

"Girl geckos?"

"Yes," Carlos says. "'Cause males would fight each other. So you can't have two males."

Bernardo's eyes widen. "Why do they fight?"

"'Cause they both want to be the boss. It's the same with dogs."

"How do you know so much?"

"I want to be a zoologist and work with animals. Or, I want to be an entomologist — someone who studies insects and learns things and maybe works for a lab or something. I've been looking stuff up."

Carlos pulls out the bottom dresser drawer and removes a towel covering a plastic container of live crickets. The container has air holes so the crickets can breathe. Their very muffled chirping gets louder. "You mustn't overfeed geckos," he says. "Crickets are the best food, vitamin-wise. We get these at the pet store. And the crickets have to be fed too. Otherwise they eat their own poop."

Bernardo's eyes widen. "What!" He looks at the crickets in the container.

"Yeah, that's the way I felt when I first heard that. So I feed the crickets stuff like a little bit of carrots or orange. Now, you don't want to give the geckos too many crickets, 'cause they won't eat them all, and then you'll have crickets that the geckos can't finish. Then you'll be hearing them chirping all night long."

Carlos sees a little smile cross Bernardo's face.

"What's so funny?"

"Nothing."

Carlos goes on. "And — listen good — don't let any crickets get away, because that happened once and we kept hearing the chirping but we couldn't find it and . . . You just don't want that to happen."

"Okay," Bernardo says. "Can I feed the geckos now?"

Carlos is still reluctant, but he gives in and hands Bernardo the container. "Keep the lid on and listen." He instructs Bernardo to open the container inside the terrarium and carefully, *carefully,* pour just a few crickets in. Unless he wants to use his hand.

Bernardo nods quickly and reaches for the container. Carlos jerks it back. "You remember what I said, right?"

"Yeah, yeah," Bernardo says.

Carlos hands him the plastic container, slowly.

Bernardo follows Carlos's instructions. He reaches into the terrarium and shakes out three crickets. Darla notices them first. Gizmo is in the cave, and Peaches is at the far end of the terrarium. Darla freezes and stares at the cricket. The cricket seems to freeze as well.

"Watch this," Carlos says. "She's real good at this."

Bernardo's mouth drops open.

Quickly, the gecko sticks out her tongue and laps up the cricket.

"*Whoa,*" Bernardo exclaims. He turns to Carlos, eyes wide.

"See?" Carlos says. "But sometimes the

geckos have to go after the cricket, and that gives them exercise."

He tells Bernardo he can feed the ants next. He might as well let him do both. The ants are much easier. Carlos shows Bernardo how to carefully remove the plastic top of the farm to sprinkle in a few cracker crumbs and then, using the eyedropper, place a few drops of water on the sand.

He breathes a sigh of relief when it all goes well. They watch the ants moving through their tunnels for a bit, and then Bernardo brushes the palms of his hands together like a person who's finished a great task and says, "I'm hungry. What's for breakfast?"

He turns and bounds down the stairs. Carlos takes a last look at his creatures and follows behind.

# Eight
## Soccer Practice

"Soccer practice after school," Mami says, handing Carlos and Bernardo sack lunches. "Make sure you're standing on the school steps, pronto. Last time, we were late, and Coach Willis wasn't too pleased." She directs them to the front door. "And don't be late to school, either."

But Bernardo has a problem with lollygagging. When they pass Rick B's Junkyard, he decides to aggravate the killer guard dog by laughing and rattling the chainlink fence until the slobbering hound is rushing it, barking and snarling.

"Ha-ha," Bernardo laughs. "That dog can't do *nothin'!*" He barks back at the dog.

"Bernardo, cut it out."

"Why? He can't get me through the fence."

"Because it's not fair to the dog."

"I don't care about being fair to the dog."

They pass Global Tire and Brakes, and Bernardo sneaks into the customer waiting room to get some gumballs out of the dispenser.

Carlos calls after him that they're going to be late, but winds up saying it to Bernardo's retreating back.

Carlos decides to continue on to school by himself.  If Bernardo gets lost, too bad. He's sick of Bernardo. He doesn't make his bed; he leaves his pajamas on the floor in the bathroom. And Carlos suspects that he's not really showering at night. *And* he leaves blobs of spitty toothpaste in the sink and doesn't rinse it out. How can anybody brush their teeth over that?

Last night, Carlos had brought up his complaints to Mami when Bernardo was out of earshot. "He's missing his mother," Mami explained.

"He doesn't act like it. When she calls, he gets off the phone real quick so he can get back to his video game."

"Be patient with him. He's your cousin. And family's important."

"I know. How can I forget?"

● ● ●

Bernardo catches up to Carlos and they reach the schoolyard just as the line-up bell rings. Bernardo gets into the line behind Carlos, chewing his gum loudly. Carlos vows to say nothing. If Bernardo gets into trouble, it'll just be too bad. No school allows gum chewing, so he won't be able to play dumb. But then Carlos thinks better of it. "You better get rid of that gum," he whispers to Bernardo. He can see Ms. Shelby-Ortiz making her way over to their line.

"What?" Bernardo says out loud.

Deja turns around and glares at him. "Shhh," she hisses. "No talking!"

Bernardo flinches. "Who's that girl?"

Carlos ignores the question. Bernardo stops the obvious chewing.

Ms. Shelby-Ortiz walks up, inspects the line, and signals for them to start for the classroom.

● ● ●

Bernardo suddenly has to make a trip to the bathroom right after school. Carlos heads to the front entrance, where Mami is probably sitting in the car, tapping the steering wheel impatiently. She's not supposed to stop right in front of the school. There's a policeman who sometimes circles the building in his patrol car at dismissal time, just so he can tell people to move along. Well, Bernardo knows where the front steps are. Better for Carlos to get out there and let Mami be annoyed with just one of them, as opposed to them both.

Carlos is happy to see that the coast is clear out front. No policeman. Mami must be running late. Bernardo saunters up just as Mami pulls in front of the school. Is the guy never in a hurry?

*o body—*

*for 41 years*
*1,573 experts*
*with 14,355*
*combined years of training*
*have failed*

*to*
*cure*
*your*
*wounds.*

*Deep inside,*

*I*
*am*
*whole.*

— *Rachel Remen, M.D.*

# Wounded
# Healers

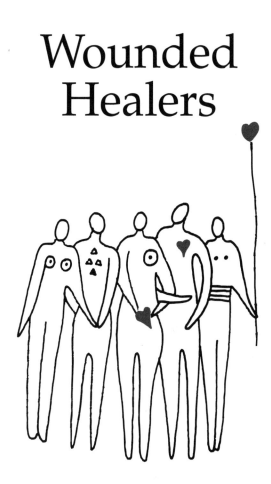

## About Poems

My poems say a truth I don't say
in any other way.
When I talk in other ways, I worry,
"Do I have my footnotes?"

Poems don't need footnotes.

Poems are from experience.

And experience
is from the heart,
not the mind.

—*Sister Rita Maginn*

God is an old man on roller skates
God is a dead cat in the road
God is protons and neutrons spinning
God is a pregnant woman with glasses
God is the unseen enemy
God is the friend (you hope)
God is this today
        that tomorrow
                something else altogether.

We put labels on things we don't understand.

        —*Nadine Parker*
         *Administrative Assistant*
         *Cancer Support Program*

*Sparrows*

The sparrows, scattered across the lawn,
are startled by some trespasser
and rise in unison.
The rush of their wings
sounds a protest against the intrusion.
Then, only yards away, they
return to their staccato search.

We unite our family's random days
to curse, to plead, to flee the sharp claws
these wayward cells have thrust
into the pattern of our lives.
We find no near refuge.
The doctor's words stalk us
even into our dreams.

—*Ellen Mauck Lessy*

## The Game

I am the keeper of pain
I keep it in its place
behind the wandering left eye
I tuck it behind the ear
like a stray lock of hair.
Half woman, half bedsheet
I sip prayers at evening, ask for medicine
and why the weeping cherry does not bloom?

Blow! they say.
I am one year old
I cannot blow this candle out
I am shy or do not try hard enough
It is a trick candle, goes out then on again.

I give the pain names:
                    burning arrow
                    claw of the eagle
I sit with it, an Indian
watching a fire—watching,
I watch it.
I am vigilant.
If I sleep it will say,
softly in the night—I have won.

—*Elizabeth Bennett*

## Give Me Strength

Give me the strength
to stay here and listen
to your story.
Help me not to run away.

Give me the freedom
to keep you close to me.

Take away that
which is unnecessary,
and give us what
we need to do Your work.

Bless the child alone tonight.
Give her trust in the morning.

*—Robin H. Lysne*
*Massage Therapist*

## In The Next Room The Doctors Talk

I wake slowly hearing voices
as I had those mornings in the summer house,
Mother and Father puttering in the garden.
I'd turn over then, drift off into
dream filled sleep.

But these are Doctors talking.
I strain to hear.
The one who wears a jacket a husband might wear
I know his voice, "I stopped doing that years ago.
I guess we all have now."
A voice I don't know, "Well it was convenient
and it worked—putting the nipple in the thigh—
good circulation. Ready if they wanted reconstruction."

I hear each word. I know where I am.
It is the day my breast will be amputated.
The Doctor will not put the nipple in my thigh
although I think, surrealist perfection,
of lifting my tennis skirt just so.

A nurse stops by, offers a sedative.
I refuse but get it anyway.
I will not have reconstruction
still I see a Doctor, scaffolding,
the Statue of Liberty. The Doctor
is climbing, nipple in his hand (he must be careful)
until he reaches her breast and with great care
he places the nipple there, right there.

Now I am in the next room
A Doctor with blood on his paper shoes
stands close by. "Ready?" he says,
"Breathe. Count 1 to 100."
I will not count.
I will say the M words: mammary,
mammogram, mass, mastectomy, metastasis, mother...

—*Elizabeth Bennett*

*Promise*

I promise you this:
I will come to you raw-boned and not filled-out
with knowing.

I promise you this:
I will come with wide eyes to bear witness.

I promise you this:
I will come with a deep and abiding faith in your wisdom.

I promise you this:
I will love myself enough to love you
from a distance you can grow in.

I promise you this:
I will tend to my own healing
so we do not stumble over my pain.

I promise you this:
in another life I was fat, full breasted,
and laughed with the moon,
And my old spirit will have her way in our hearts.

—*Ginny Buzzell, Ph.D.*
*Psychotherapist*

## Hippocratic Oath

May I escape
the shame, inadequacy, self-judgement and self-doubt
my teachers have taught me.

May I trust
that my love is as needed as my knowledge.

May I remember
in me, the limitations of every man.

May I be open
to know my darkness and true to what light I have.

May I be used
as a blessing and a friend to life.

—*Rachel Remen, M.D.*

*Deeper Than Bone*

Doctor's office. On a screen
X-Rays of my mother,
the first time I see her
inside out:

pelvic bones,
my cradle before birth.
rib cage,
sheltering her heart.

Doctor says,
"Notice extreme curvature of spine."

I know that curve—
bent from washing other people's floors,
hours spent at sewing machine
turning hems into food.

"Notice how her bladder sags
right to pelvic floor—
Cystocele", he calls it,
from bearing too many children.

Doctor writes his notes, dispenses pills.
His charts don't show
mother  wife  widow.

Through X-ray glow
he sees inside
yet not inside enough:

only the
bones
show.

> —*Chaya Blitzer*
> *Daughter*

## Practice

The living and dying happens today;
Please open my eyes to the truth of this moment.

—*David Teegarden, M.D.*
*Family Practice*

♥

## Examining Room

As I enter into this new space
May I see and be seen.
May I touch and be touched.
May I speak and be spoken to.
May I feel and be felt.
May I experience and be experienced
That we may both become whole.

—*Carole Milligan, M.D.*
*Radiation Oncologist*

What is my truth?
I have always felt it
But had trouble with the words.
Maybe that's because
I too was told to be quiet.

I think my truth was once
a loud, exuberant child,
But now it dwells in my heart
And brings tears to my eyes
When I hear other people's poems.

—*Shannon McGowan M.F.C.C.*
*Director, Wellness Community*

## The Bowl and the Stones

I was given a small Chinese Bowl
not much larger than a silver dollar.

The woman who gave it to me came
from England.
She had seen World War II.
She emerged suspicious, hard of hearing
and cruel.
But, when she saw the bowl, she thought
it was right for me.
She said, "It's a place where you can store
all of your hostilities."

Now that bowl holds five tiny stones,
enough to fill it.
Four of the stones,
of different colors,
were given to me by a young woman
who came to cry on my porch.
The fifth stone,
larger than the others,
is round and pure as alabaster.
This one I gave to myself.
It presented itself
among thousands of grey beach rocks.
This one was mine, for it held
the secret wish, the one I had, unknowingly,
gone there to find.

—Cora Boyd Silva

## The Meeting

The scientists came late at night
And spoke in soft, subdued tones
About their work. Hushed reverence
For their breakthroughs.
They would like to try a new drug.
Low risks, high gain.
Certain tradeoffs—
　　"Do we have your consent?
　　Can we answer any questions?
　　Do you understand?"
The hushed, subdued emotionless voices.
The immediacy of preparation for battle.
What I understand is her fear.
The big bed with the sides up,
Moving down the shiny floor.

　　　　　　　　　—Joan Beesley
　　　　　　　　　Mother

## A Professional's Goodbye And Thanks

I thank the children
For showing me how to best help them,
For leading the way,
For teaching me how to listen to their real needs,
For helping me gain the courage and the strength
    of heart
To follow them to the threshold of life
With the childlike openness of heart
That alone can see clearly from there.
For helping me live more and more by the love and light
    of life
So that we would not turn away from what was difficult
    to face or to bear,
But continued on together,
Sharing the treasures of heart
Which allow burdens to be carried more lightly,
Fears to fade in the dawn of inner knowing,
The heart itself to be uplifted from outer sorrow
    to inner peace.

I thank the parents
For sharing their children with me,
For sharing their own hearts with me
As we walked through the fire together,
For teaching me how to survive and to gain
    inner strength from personal crisis,
For mounting the courage to take the children home
    whenever that was appropriate—
Even if the move was a step into the unknown.
For loving their children selflessly enough
    to set them free when that was needed.

—Lee Horsman, R.N.

## But Not Today

Sometimes
I can let go of the past,
a past locked behind the doors
of painful memories.
But not today.

Sometimes
I can accept the reality
that is me
and journey headlong
into the unknown.
But not today.
Today change comes hard.
I wear my feelings
on my sleeve,
and nothing seems right.

Sometimes
I feel I can
weather anything
tackle anything
do anything.
But not today.

—Brenda Neal

## Truth

I'm such a humble beginner.
God's love is always within me
but I can only allow myself
to feel it for a few minutes at a time.
Then thoughts come in of a
plane ticket, Jerry's herbs, and
pleasures of the flesh.

—*Alice Large*

## Self Portrait

There stands the old olive tree
Her trunk a gnarled witness to the years.
A thing not of beauty but of strength—
Of integrity.
The scars tell a story.

She has grown her share of fruit over the years
Which yields oil for light and nourishment
Rewarding labor
But olives are bitter:
"You have to develop a taste for them"
Many don't.  "Why bother?"

Creatures are hiding
in the shelter of her branches—
Many, many.
The tree loves them all.

She is still growing, that old tree—
More slowly, much more slowly.
It hurts to grow—it takes so much effort.
But grow she must.

How deep do the roots go?
How wide?
There is no telling.
Some inevitable day when she falls, dying,
Perhaps the hidden sources will be seen,
Briefly,
Before her essence rejoins the earth
That gave her birth.

—Ursula Growald

## Self Doubt

At age ten I drew
a beautiful woman
on the chalkboard.
She had breasts and tiny waist
and long hair and a gown.
As I stood back to savor
my art, I needed
no one to tell me
how wonderful she was.
It didn't even matter
that the teacher would
soon erase my drawing
and fill up that space
with numbers or history
or homework assignments.
Just the creation
of my beautiful woman
had been enough.
My struggle in healing has been
to let my ten-year-old create again.

—*Carol Munson*

## Change

A feeling hardened
into a belief. It was
heavy and solid
and immovable.
Cold as ice.
hard as steel. Tight
as a clenched jaw.

It was so deep, so long, so old.
Talking about it reinforced it
like earthquake proofing,
making my throat bloody and sore.

I brought it, like a sculpture,
out into nature and set it
in the garden
underneath a tree.

Feelings change unless they harden.
Wind in your leaves, teach me.

> —*Jnani Chapman, R.N.*
> *Massage Therapist*

*Mother Knows Best...*

Don't talk
about your troubles.
No one loves a sad face.

O Mom.

The truth is
cheer isolates,
humor defends,
competence intimidates,
control separates,
and sadness...

sadness opens us to each other.

—*Rachel Remen, M.D.*

## A Geography of My Scars

In the east, a railroad track running
from the valley of my arm
to the hilltop of my breast.
In the west, a creekbed curving
along the ridge of a rib.
It is not a perfect landscape—unfit for
postcards, calendars
or brochures. But my husband is blind
to the surface flaws, and I see myself
through his eyes: the eyes of a native
who overlooks things
that only a tourist would notice.

—Cheryl Parsons Darnell

*Chemotherapy*

Women in headscarves—
The clear, clean poetry of cheekbone
The magnetic depth of eyes
The heart-stopping shape of faces
The elegant curve of the neck.
Women in headscarves—
Grieving for their hair.

—*Rachel Remen, M.D.*

In the middle of the night
My blood line drips.
Drops of life are trickling in
As life itself ebbs, in the same instant.
My body is hard at work
Deceiving me by building the wrong cells—
Cancer cells, leukemia—
Like a raging forest fire with no rain in sight,
Out of control.

If living organisms try to heal, why is my body
Doing the opposite?
It has no respect for my authority,
My artillery of powerful visualizations,
My prayers and those of many others.
Is there no water to squelch this fire?
No way to put it out?

—*Deborah Smith*

## Stewardship

In weighted sleep, the light burns down
and we are called to tend the glow,
With cupped hands and kindling breath.
To love the embers as the flame,
To guard from cold and dampened wind
a spark which may yet flare again.
Let not our hands unmindful be
so long as any fire remains.

—*Ann Worley, J.D.*
*Hospital Administrator*

*Beach Flowers*

How tough the beach flowers have to be—
Bright yellow, scarlet pink, little flags of purple.
They grip the earth down close
And hang on for dear life
While winds sweep in from outer space
And pound them
On their way around the world.

I thought:
I am a flower
A strong one.
And this must be
The neighborhood
Where I grew up.

I must have been a blue one
With a simple yellow middle.
I must have dug out wide, not deep,
And pushed my roots through sharp sand.
I must have searched for water

Through many scorching days.
I must have quivered in the dark
With no knowledge of morning,
And no hope.
I must have ached with loneliness
Before I found a way,
With silence, to speak.

Me, buffeted.
One, two over there,
Buffeted and torn by the wind.
Some blew away; some died.
But always there were new blooms,
And sometimes,
When the wind died down,
We could rest our faces in the sun
And swoon with the sweet smells of spring.

It took years for me
To learn we were a garden
And finally hear
The music of the sea.

—*Susan Lipsett*

## Growing Old

I never thought I would grow old
But rather, like my father, die before my time
(But what is anyone's time?)
At any rate, not like his protracted, painful course
But quick, a short stroke, perhaps, or aneurysm
Of which I would be totally unaware
Except for the final moment
When I would bestow upon my grieving daughters
My final wise words
which they would carry with them forever
After I had drifted into another world, with no pain,
no regrets.

How could I have known
When I was twenty, or thirty, or even forty
That one day I would feel my body slowing dying,
A stiff neck that lasts for days, no, weeks
Sagging breasts that pull me down
A slowing heart that risks too little
Eyes that see poorly in the dark,
that do not wish to see too much.

Gray hair, a few wrinkles—I expected those
But not the brown spots on my crinkled hands
Not the sinus pains from vintage wine.

Never the new fear of downhill skiing,
of cantering on horseback
of diving into sea waves.

My body has made me a coward
By showing the truth
I once found impossible to believe.
My body and I are one.
We are in this together.
We will soon vanish, together.

—*Pauline Stein*

*rachelpoems*

Pain.
I give you
the gift
of my not-knowing.

Thank you, body.
Without you
I would be
too vague
to hug.

Integrity
is letting go
of what was never yours.

Pain.
I am alive.

—*Rachel Remen, M.D.*

Tomorrow will awaken me
with that morning slap of nausea.
It will be no early and accustomed sign
of nurture, flesh of my flesh,
but a stranger tracking
through my veins,
search-and-destroy chemistry:
the caustic midwife of my future.

I must learn
to love this fire,
bless each translucent drop
and know some sacrament of grace
among the IV's and the alcohol.
I pray.
I long for the heaven
of a half-century
and my children grown.

—*Ellen Mauck Lessy*

## The Hunter

Held motionless and still,
Pinned against the sky
And then released to plummet,
Swerve, lazily drift by:
Tracking across the meadow,
Faded and dusty brown...
Banking, turning, dipping
Inches above the ground,
Then suddenly, thrusting skyward
(Some small thing has died)...
Curving around the shoreline,
So the hawk, with hunter's pride,
Soars across my thinking,
Leaving me cold inside.

—*Nancy B. Frank*


## Hawk

Wide-winged, the hawk
Explodes out of the stillness...
From absolute silence... suddenly...
Like a scream
From the misty, mysterious,
Towering pines...
It pounces... soars... is gone.
Then all is almost as before...
Almost.

—*Nancy B. Frank*

Healing is soaring like the hawk over the meadow
    filtering through the pines
    whistling with the wind
    pounding with the sea as it rolls to the beach
    swirling on the sand among the shore birds
And then listening still in the silence
to the deep deep place within
That cries for the freedom to live.

        *—Elinor Montgomery*

*In Your Sleep*

In your sleep
You throw your arm over my shoulder
And your hand rests
Where my right breast
Used to be.

So, the nerves reconnect
The flesh knits
And the ache quiets.

A friend told me
She feels pain
In her missing breast.
It may be the same thing, but
I have started to call
What I feel in mine
Sort of like love.

*—Judith Lowry*

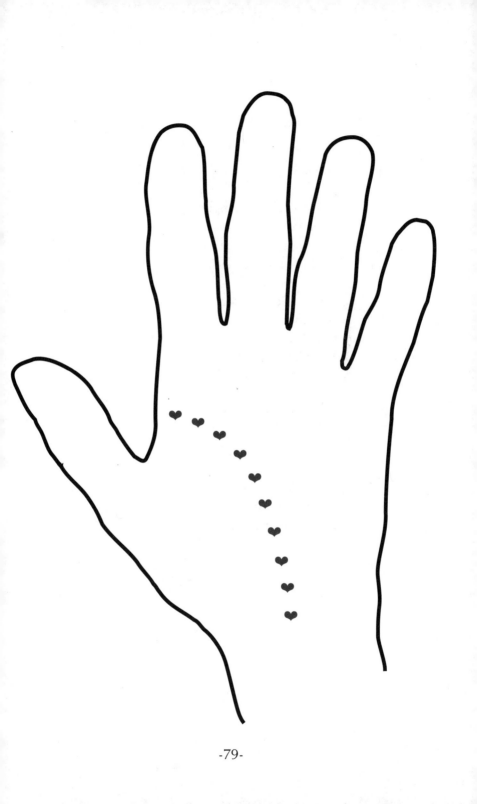

❤ ───────────────────────────────────────────

## Round Up the Usual Suspects

I suspect that the hope
to be more than I am
will never leave me.
And the temptation
to be less than I
am will never cease.
And the struggle
to live without
harm between the
more and the less
will never subside.
And that when I die
or get clear
in all this
I'll see the joke
but with too much
compassion to laugh
at my own expense.

—Michael Lerner
*Health Educator*

## The Old Neighborhood

The Teacher says:
"We are Beings of Light"
For him, a truth
For me, a hope

I know myself
By means of wounds
Familiar pain....
        "I'm not enough"
        "I don't belong"

The comfort
of the old neighborhood...
Take the usual right at
        "Nobody cares"
A left at the corner of Judgement and Jealousy
Past three old rejections,
        "Too smart"
        "Too strong"
        "Too intimidating"
leaning together, like a row of Victorian houses.
And then we're home.

—*Rachel Remen, M.D.*

## Child

The birch tree falls between us,
We can't agree about the lake;
The dogs are on her side.
We don't foresee the easy give and take
Of a forty-year friendship;
the habit of wariness is too strong for that.

And yet, for forty years I have sustained her.
And now her fierce form stands
Between the wind and me.

—Jane Carroll

*Thanksgiving Eve 1985*

Chemotherapy day, Wednesday—
The children come home from college,
tired, cross, all of us shifting gears.
A good meal—warm and soothing, a good night's sleep.
The next day I lined them up,
dressed in their best for church.
I picked over their clothes like a mother cat with her kittens.
Skip in a bow tie from Dad's closet,
Rawls, dark socks from Skip's dresser,
Kay, looking beautiful in an Austrian skirt and sweater,
I take their picture on the front porch.
They are growing up nicely.
Let me live to see my children's children, Lord.

—*Carol W. Costenbader*

*Lumpectomy*

Re-shaped to the proportions of a more delicate woman
this breast snubs my attentions,
while the other, robustly filling its cup of the bra,
hints that our newcomer isn't really a breast.
I wish to welcome my new flesh,
but its nipple saucily staring as if due a younger woman,
says it won't have that.
Hardened by x-ray, needles, knives, drains, and radium scorch
it clings coldly to my alien chest.

I'm shy with this still,
respecting our maiming and my confused vanity,
wondering at my tenderness to its cruelty,
not thinking how I could have died of it.

—*Mary Grow*

## First Bath

I bend to the warm bath
I will fill it with my body,
practice a kind of deception,
displacing the same amount of water as before.
Not wanting all the pleasure at once,
I place one foot, then the other
submit to its warmth.
Just as before, the water
Finds its way around the body.
I slide down deeper; where there is breast
water flows around it.
Where there is none, I make
small waves, cupping my hand.
As if I hold a conch shell to my ear
the water lapping gently, whispers
listen, lapping, listen, whispers
survival, survival.

—Elizabeth Bennett

# In the Hospital

When they came at me with sharp knives
I put perfume under my nose.

When they knocked me out on the
operating table
I dreamed I was flying.

When they asked me embarrassing questions
I remembered the clouds in the sky.

When they were about to drown me
I floated.

When they laid harsh hands on me
I thought of fireworks I had seen with you.

When they told me I was sick and might die
I left them and went away with you
to where I live

When they took off my right breast
I gave it to them.

—*Patricia Goedicke*

There is not enough time in any day for the body,
this much I have known, but never as I know it now.
Today I saw grass moving across a hill like green fire,
and there was tenderness also,
the purple lupine and orange poppy covering this same hill
and yes a stream with water forming the small valley.
I sat until I could hear the bees
I could see the grass moving like the hair moves on the head
of someone you love...
The body said, "Leave the path and walk up the stream."
The body said, "Sit on the breast warm rock and rest..."
I did this, and I loved the surface of the earth.

It is true I almost died.
Just four months ago there were so many bruises traveling up
        both arms
that they changed the intravenous sites every four hours
        desperately
I could no longer recognize my own hands.

At night, they finally came and put the life lines into my neck,
they turned me upside down to do this necessary next thing,
each day brought a new necessity,
day after day I did not know my hand,
this body,
hair unwashed
this body
changed forever
but there were small details even then that begged for entry.

Mother bathing me each morning with hospital rough
        washcloths
but with such tenderness and wish for warm water
that my skin did not hurt, it moved out towards her,
        recognizing at last its own

a trust that went deeper than peril,
her force becoming mine
but in surprising ways...
It was the cream she put under my eyes each morning,
believing that there would be a time again that I would
care about beauty
believing in this body when I could not.

There is a time each day when I am frightened.
Moving in and out of sleep can be treacherous,
can bring that other world close again

when only nurses came,
after my parents left exhausted,
after the last call to Dave,
after the Bach lute suites had played themselves out,
and the pain and sleeplessness kept coming...
I knew what it meant to depend on the good will of strangers.
Life moves suddenly and drastically outside the safety of love

And there is peril
There is peril
But it turns in surprising ways
it brings you close up to the face of things
right up near as can be
where all life begs to enter

> —Dorian Ross, Ph.D.
> Therapist

## Session

You tell me of your mother's fear,
the great navigator of your life.

It whispered to you,
"Follow me, don't go away to school."
You followed it.

It whispered to you,
"Follow me, don't marry him"
You followed it.

It whispered to you,
"Follow me, the lump will go away"
You followed it.

You lay it down between us
on the rug.
We look at it together.
Now, with one breast
and nothing left to lose.
Finally, you can begin.

—*Rachel Remen, M.D.*

*Group*

May I sit with wisdom and compassion
        at the ancient fires
        of dashed hopes
        and lost dreams.

May the pain which brings us together
        become the cave we enter
        in reverent descent
           and surrender
                to what Is.

May we have the courage
        to bear this rebirth together.

               —*Carol Howard, M.F.C.C.*
                *Therapist, Support Group Leader*

## The Bravest Heart

A hummingbird sat on my finger,
Fractured jewel the cat brought in.

Sitting on my finger
Softly, calmly preening its one good wing.

Lifting its beak to accept
a drop of sugar water,
The only hope I had to offer.

Little bird, how can it be that you,
So small, so broken,
can face the giant
With so bright an eye, so brave a heart?

—*Susan Chernak*

## The Lesson of Texas

I grew up in Texas
where you grow accustomed
to sudden weather
Where rains that pour while
the sun still shines
do not surprise you
Where northers that mar
the sky like a bruise
do not surprise you
Where floods that wash
up rattlesnakes
do not surprise you
Where droughts that crack
the skin of the earth
do not surprise you
Where hurricanes that
blow the Gulf inland
do not surprise you
Where twisters that eat
houses for breakfast
do not surprise you
I grew up in Texas
where you learn to keep candles
and flashlight batteries
Where you learn about
weather, love and life
and how to ride it out.

—*Cheryl Parsons Darnell*

## A Young Man Dies Early In The Afternoon

He is sitting, leaning forward.
His head resting heavy,
elbows supporting the enormous weight
of his continued consciousness

Eyes glazed with the effort of too many nights of catching
himself
before he falls too far asleep

His breathing is labored, heavy grasping at a pittance of air,
gurgling, choking but
still breathing.

His body is gaunt but heavy with the accumulation
of unspent fluids, his belly distended, huge and weildy

His legs two weeping pillars of inert but sensate flesh.

His eyes wild with the glory of his will.

—*Cathy McFann, M.F.C.C.*
*Hospice*

## Pain

There is a spot on my back
where a wing is growing.
No one knows it's there
but I am awakened in the night
by the birds sitting on the wire
and waiting for my flight.
They know
I know.

—*Fraser MacBeth*

They come in a seemingly endless stream,
The tiny ones, the sick ones, the broken ones.

The father prays for a miracle,
That his son will be cured.

The mother prays for hope,
That her son will beat the odds and survive.

The grandfather cries in anguish
"Doc, I don't even know what to pray for."

And I, I simply ask,
"Help me to do what is right."

—*Norma Hirsch, M.D.*
*Neonatologist*

Teach me how to honor this day
How to walk among the billowing sheets of sunlight
Arm in arm with the brilliant angel of death
How to find my home with a fire in the hearth
In the green, green fields of this life.

—*Vivekan Flint*
*Cancer Research Associate*

*The Truth*

There's this
Enchanted forest
with a needle
carpet
And a large owl
in an opportune tree
And along the path
green and purple
Thistle
with orange
Butterflies
on them
then
I am not sorry

*—Don Martin*

Walking through the enchanted forest
he shows me an owl in a tree
Overlooking the ocean from the cliff
he points to the Raven circling
Out our window he shows me
        the woodpecker
Down the road, the fat unknown
perhaps a sparrow puffed large
against the wind.

His pain is not my pain.
That is my pain.

>                    —*Joan Martin*
>                    *Wife*

*Family*

His Holiness said:
I hope these words I've spoken today
Have been worthwhile—
But if not.... it doesn't matter....
I cling to the string on my neck
That he left,
And I wonder.

Tears hang behind my eyes
like fog hangs off the beach
spilling forward... just...
as I imagine myself out of range,
they wash loose the grief and the dust
of the corners and soften
all the edges of pain.

In the dark here
I remember your loving hugs,
urging me on.
I still can see you gathered,
—such an unlikely family—
and I know I can find
my way home.

—Christine Saxton

## Help With Healing

Powerful prayers sent to me by
      friends, relatives, and strangers
Loving bear hugs from Willie, Jason,
      Coby, Seth, Aaron and Alicia
Ingesting thousands of words and
      wisdom in books
Practicing peace and calmness in the
      midst of chaos
Learning to take time for me
Pondering the wonders of nature
Forcing myself to "Be Here Now"
Letting go of fears and worry
as Alicia lets go of a
helium balloon and marvels at
the wonder of it.

—*Beverly Buckle*

## One More Time

Next morning, at the Medical Center
Though the X-ray Room swallows me whole,

Though cold crackles in the corridors
I brace myself against it and then relax.

Lying there on the polished steel table
I step right out of my body,

Suspended in icy silence
I look at myself from far off
Calmly, I feel free

Even though I'm not, now
Or ever:

the metal teeth of Death bite
But spit me out

One more time:

When the technician says breathe
I breathe.

—*Patricia Goedicke*

*Trail to Winnemucca in June*
*(One Year After Cancer Treatment)*

Columbine graces the granite
mountain streams tumble,
then rest in dark pools
the snow patch melts and trickles
mud oozes under my foot
you can slide a finger
deep in this garden
way up to the third knuckle.

Last summer's parched path
couldn't be penetrated an inch
boots crunched on dry gravel
my spirit dry as the faded phlox
fear of recurrence higher than the fire danger
no assumptions about another spring.

Today on this trail meadows
lush with mule ears and lupine—
so green I could shout.

— *Ann Davidson*

## Prayer

Open my heart that I may be open.
Open my eyes that I may see.
Guide my wisdom
that it may be used in fruitful ways.
Guide my love
that it may flow freely
to and from those in need.
Guide my hands
that they find and touch
the parts that need healing
Guide my feet
that they stay on the true path.
Let me use the gifts I have.

—*Jan Chambers, M.D.*
*Obstetrician/Gynecologist*

Creator—
You have instilled in me a rainbow
for your children to walk on
to see and experience You.
Open my heart,
that the fullness of light and color
be reflected in me.
Remind me of the joy I feel in Your presence.
Comfort me when clouds block the light
and I cannot see the colors within.
When I am disheartened,
bring me to your pot of gold
that I might see again with new eyes,
Trust again the purpose of my service with You
Hope again in Your love
for all your children
and the earth.

—*Marilyn Wall, N.P.*
*Aids Clinic*

## Honed Stone

a squadron of pelicans fly
in formation
above my head
their shadows momentarily
block the sun
as i slowly walk the beach edge
where dark wet sand arcs
into dry light
where waves deposit
the ocean leftovers
bit of kelp
piece of shell
once jagged stone
honed to a smooth disc

oh God, smooth the
burrs of bitterness
off my soul
burnish the fear
from my heart
polish the edges
of my anger
make me
the glistening smooth stone
that feels good in your hand
take me home
and place me on your mantel

—Keith Smith
Husband

*In The Hospital*

The only thing of beauty that my eyes behold
Is a vase of cut flowers from my love
This alone is my focal point in a world gone mad
These flowers are my life line to sanity
Through them I know there is wonder and loveliness
The love that sent them is sufficient to cling to
for the moment.

—*Deborah Smith*

## Gift From Denise

Her mother died
Of breast cancer
When Denise was 24,
Too young to know her task then
Was to separate
From mother,
Like any girl,
Too young to know
It was natural
To draw back
From illness and approaching death,
Too young to know
To ask the questions
She later yearned
For answers to.

My daughter at 22
Asks me nothing
About how it feels
To have one breast,
What thoughts,
Emerge in the dark.
My daughter
Asks me nothing
About how it was
When she and I were young.
She approaches cautiously now
After a long silence.
I speak to her gently
In measured sentences
Offering memories and feelings
Without judgment,
Sharing glimpses of myself,
Hoping she will accept these gifts,
String them together
And wear them later
Like a necklace of pearls.

—*Ann Davidson*

" 3 A.M. "

Awake again at 3 A.M.
Black Elk said:
"He knows wisdom
who sees the morning star."
I should be wise enough
By now.
I use the time to write down
The recent doings of my daughter
An odd turn of phrase
A new joke
Her obsession with the piano.
Already going places I've never been,
she has written three songs
And I record their names.
I describe a habit she has
Of emitting sudden shrieks
At seemingly random times.

I've heard that sound before.
Once dancing at a gay bar, wild times,
Where some held whistles between their teeth
And periodically a strong blast
Summarized the scene.

And again in a roundhouse
Chaw-se
Indian Grinding Rock
3 A.M. and half of us are asleep
And half are watching dancers
In tule aprons
And rabbitskin capes.
Boys rush in and the head drummer blows
His elderberry whistle.
"Wake up," he says "and see
The new ones coming."

Now these calls to life
Startle me in my kitchen
On the porch, by the couch
And I write it all down
That she may know
By what loving eyes she has been seen
Now that the rattlesnake
Has called me
To the dance.

—*Judith Lowry*

## Until You Were Gone

I didn't know
how strong my love for you was
until you were gone.
I never really told you how much I loved you.
I didn't know
how precious life is
until you were gone.
You made me realize nothing should be taken for
granted.

I didn't know
what all your sayings meant
until you were gone,
but now I see.
I "live each day to the fullest",
I "make it easy", I "make it fun",
and I "keep on keeping on".

I didn't know
how much you meant to me
until you were gone.
You taught me everything, my teacher,
my friend.

I didn't know
how important memories are
until you were gone.
Memories are all I have now.
I cherish every one.

I didn't know
how hard it would be to lose you
until it happened.
I miss you more than anything.
I just didn't know.

—*Alice Stewart*
*Daughter*

Because it grows in
your heart.
My love will live
even after I am gone.

—*Chris McDonald*

God—
Guide me to be open.
Connect my mind and my heart.
Let me hear with clear ears
And speak with true voice.
Teach me to trust.
Let my intention be loving
And may this love offer healing wisdom.
Help me to be in the light
And open my eyes to see in the darkness
To do good work today.

—*Mark Wexman, M.D.*
*Cardiologist*

In a place of stillness,
the one who thinks
hears the whisper of the heart.

In a place of trust,
the one who cures,
heals.

In a place of acceptance,
a stone
can explode
into a butterfly.

*—Rachel Remen, M.D. and Vivekan Flint*
*I.S.H.I.*

*Loss*

Sometimes,
when the white mist stirs
among the boughs
of the mournful trees,
the egret unfurls
her prayerful wings
and floats into a sky
the color of tears.
She loves the idea of her life
as much as I love mine
but understands as little
as I about the pain
that makes the idea real.

I ask: How can I love this life
knowing before it ends
I will have to lose everything
I hold most dear?
And I wonder if the egret long mourns
the fledgling which has fallen
delicate as a snowflake
frightened and fluttering hopelessly
into the damp unknown?

Does she carry the thorn that pierces
deeper than bone
even as she goes earnestly about
the work of living in this world?

Perhaps, but I think, too,
that the little slip of a fish
that just went whole and wriggling
down her long muscular throat
is everything she could have wanted
in this precious moment
of her short, uncertain life.

*—Vivekan Flint*
*Cancer Research Associate*